Yuvi's Candy Tree

To Yuvi, whose life inspired this story – L.S.

For Erin, Jeff, and Jude – J.L.P.

KAR-BEN Publishing
A division of Lerner Publishing Group, Inc.
241 First Avenue North
Minneapolis, MN 55401 U.S.A.
1-800-4KARBEN

Website address: www.karben.com

Library of Congress Cataloging-in-Publication Data

Simpson, Lesley.
    Yuvi's candy tree / by Lesley Simpson ; illustrated by Janice Lee Porter.
        p.   cm.
    Summary: Fleeing famine in her native Ethiopia, five-year-old Yuvi is sure she will have a candy tree when she arrives in Jerusalem.
    ISBN 978-0-7613-5651-6 (lib. bdg. : alk. paper)
    [1. Emigration and immigration—Fiction. 2. Trees—Fiction. 3. Jews—Ethiopia—Fiction. 4. Ethiopia—Fiction. 5. Israel—Fiction.] I. Porter, Janice Lee, ill. II. Title.
    PZ7.S6065Yu 2011
    [E]—dc22   2010003880

Manufactured in the United States of America
1 - DP - 11/1/10

Yuvi's Candy Tree

By Lesley Simpson

Illustrated by Janice Lee Porter

KAR-BEN
PUBLISHING

I escaped on a donkey in the dark.
I wore my white dress with embroidered flowers.

I rode on a donkey because I was only five.
I had no shoes.

My aunts whispered about robbers.
I was afraid of the hyena's screech.
At night we ran.
Our dresses whooshed in the wind.

My grandmother told me not to be afraid.
"We are going to Jerusalem. We have angels with us.
We'll fly home."

During the day we slept under trees, hiding.
My dress turned the color of dirt.
We played Shabbat by packing mud into pretend dabu,
our Ethiopian bread.
We slurped make-believe coffee made of stones.

We pretended to be mothers, showering our cousins
with pebbles.
My mother was already in Jerusalem with my baby brother.
Now it was my turn.

My grandmother made a harness so I would not fall off.
I waved to the moon and stars, snuggled under the
donkey's belly.
"We are going to Jerusalem," said my grandmother.
"We have angels with us. We'll fly home."

I did not see angels.
I saw only sand.

Wind whipped the sand into my mouth.
I was thirsty.

I dreamed of candy. Once my father brought it from the
market, hard and white, small and sweet.

"We are going to our real home, to Israel," said my grandmother. "In Jerusalem, your wishes will come true,"

But the next morning I saw men.
"Robbers!" I cried.

We had money hidden in the hems of our clothes.
But the robbers tore at the hems, grabbed the money, and ran.

We hid most of the money we had left in the babies' backpacks.
More robbers came. They stole the backpacks.

We had a tiny bit of money left, tucked under the donkey's blanket.
"Hide the money in the donkey's cheeks," I suggested.
"Yuvi, the donkey will eat it," said my grandmother.

"We're going to Jerusalem. We have angels with us.
We'll fly home," said my grandmother.
"We'll be back," the robbers said, laughing as they rode away.

"Then hide the money in my cheeks,"
I said, opening my mouth.
"Yuvi, you might eat it!" said my
grandmother.
I hid the money under my curls.
"Clever girl," said my grandmother.

The robbers came back.
They pulled at our torn hems.
They looked in our empty backpacks.
"No money," we said.

I was afraid they could see through my curls.
"The robbers are not as smart as you," whispered
my grandmother. "We are going to Jerusalem.
We have angels with us. We'll fly home."

We ran many nights.
We slept many days.
My feet bled.

We drank from the muddy river.

My tummy ached.

Finally we arrived at the refugee camp.

The next week we climbed the stairs to a big airplane.
People pushed and shoved.
The engine's roar hurt my ears.
My grandmother held my hand.
I patted my head and felt the money.
My grandmother winked.

"In Jerusalem there will be candy, clothes, and games," she said.
"And as much bread as you can eat."
I imagined orchards of candy trees. You could eat as much
as you wanted, and the candy would grow back.
I imagined bread in my hands, bread stuffed into my pockets,
and pillows of bread.

White women on the airplane poured milk. They were the
first white people I had ever seen, and I thought they were
angels. They poured spoonfuls of medicine into my mouth.
They wrapped my feet in soft bandages. Their voices were
soft. In the desert we were thirsty. Here they poured us big
glasses of water. "Am I in heaven?" I asked the white angel.

"You are going to Jerusalem," she said. "You are
going home."
"Do you have wings?" I asked the angel.
"Yes!" she said, flapping her arms.

There was a hush on the plane when we landed in Israel.
We made our way through the busy airport and onto a bus.
We were going to Jerusalem.
I looked out the window.
"What is that?" I asked.

"Orange trees," said the bus driver.
"What happens if you pick an orange?" I asked.
"They grow back. Eat as many as you want," said the driver.
"Juicy and sweet."
Now I understood.
But the bus driver had the name wrong.

I had found my candy tree.

AFTERWARD

Yuvi's Candy Tree is a fictional story based on the true story of Yuvi Tashome. Yuvi's full name was Yeuvmert which, in Amharic, the language of Ethiopia, means "a good or beautiful product." Yuvi was given a Hebrew name when she moved to Israel, but to recover her history, she reclaimed her Ethiopian name, shortening it to Yuvi.

Yuvi escaped from Ethiopia to a Sudanese refugee camp when she was a little girl. She was later airlifted to Israel as part of Operation Moses, one of several Israeli rescue operations of Ethiopian Jews in the 1980s and 1990s. Israel's Law of Return gives Jews of all countries the right to return to Israel. The Ethiopian Jews viewed Israel as their home, and they risked their lives to return. Thousands died on the way.

I first met Yuvi during the holiday of Passover, when Jews traditionally tell the story of the Israelites' Biblical exodus from Egypt. The Passover story is about what it means to be a slave and what it means to be free. When Yuvi told me her story, I felt as if the Haggadah was coming alive before my eyes.

With this book I honor her story, and celebrate her life.

--*Lesley Simpson*

ABOUT THE AUTHOR

Lesley Simpson is a Canadian journalist and children's author. Her first article, "What To Do When You Can't Fall Asleep And Have Run Out Of Flashlight Batteries" was published in a Canadian anthology when she was an 11-year-old insomniac. She's the illustrator and author of *The Hug* (Annick Press), as well as the author of *The Shabbat Box* and *The Purim Surprise* (Kar-Ben). Lesley has taught journalism and creative writing at Canadian universities. She lives in Toronto, Canada.

ABOUT THE ILLUSTRATOR

Janice Lee Porter was born and raised in Chicago. She has a BFA in painting from Kansas City Art Institute, and her MFA degree from California State University, Chico. She is the illustrator of over two dozen children's books. She is an art faculty member at Shasta College in Redding, CA., where she teaches painting and drawing. She lives in Chico, California.